Hairy Maclary's

Rumpus at the Vet

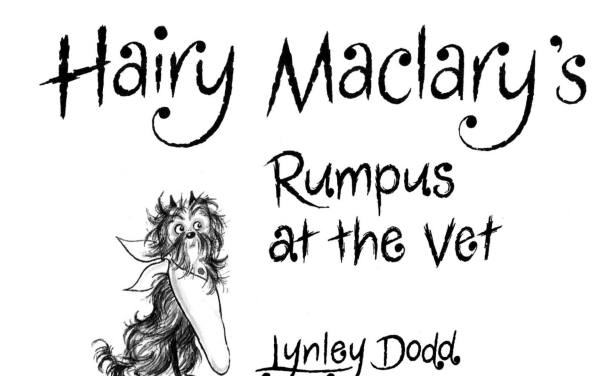

Lynley Dodd

PUFFIN BOOKS

Down at the Vet's
there were all kinds of pets,
with troubles and woes
from their ears to their toes.
Sniffles and snuffles
and doses of flu,
itches and stitches
and tummy ache too.
So many animals,
watchful and wary,
and Hairy Maclary
from Donaldson's Dairy.

There were miserable dogs,
cantankerous cats,
a rabbit with pimples
and rickety rats.
Mice with the sneezes,
a goat in a rage,
and Cassie the cockatoo
locked in her cage.

Cassie had claws
and a troublesome beak.
She saw something twitch
so she gave it a
TWEAK.

She pulled it so hard
that she plucked out a hair
and Hairy Maclary
jumped high in the air.

A bowl full of mice
was bundled about.
Over it went
and the mice tumbled out.

Four fussy budgies
with Grandmother Goff
flew out of their cage
when the bottom dropped off.

Grizzly MacDuff
with a bottlebrush tail
leaped out of his basket
and over the rail.

The Poppadum kittens
from Parkinson Place
squeezed through an opening
and joined in the chase.

Barnacle Beasley
forgot he was sore.
He bumbled and clattered
all over the floor.

Then Custard the labrador,
Muffin McLay
and Noodle the poodle
decided to play.
They skidded and scampered,
they slid all around
and bottles and boxes
came tumbling down.

What a kerfuffle,
a scramble of paws,
a tangle of bodies,
a jumble of jaws.
With squawking and yowling
and mournful miaow,
they really were making
a TERRIBLE row.

Out came the Vet.
'I'll fix them,' she said.
But she tripped on a lead
and fell over instead.

Geezer the goat
crashed into a cage.
He butted the bars
in a thundering rage.

Cassie got mad.
She rattled her beak.
She saw something twitch
so she
gave
it
a ....

TWEAK.

PUFFIN BOOKS

Published by the Penguin Group
Penguin Books Ltd, 80 Strand, London WC2R 0RL, England
Penguin Group (USA) Inc., 375 Hudson Street, New York, New York 10014, USA
Penguin Group (Canada), 10 Alcorn Avenue, Toronto, Ontario, Canada M4V 3B2 (a division of Pearson Penguin Canada Inc.)
Penguin Ireland, 25 St Stephen's Green, Dublin 2, Ireland (a division of Penguin Books Ltd)
Penguin Group (Australia), 250 Camberwell Road, Camberwell, Victoria 3124, Australia (a division of Pearson Australia Group Pty Ltd)
Penguin Books India Pvt Ltd, 11 Community Centre, Panchsheel Park, New Delhi – 110 017, India
Penguin Group (NZ), cnr Airborne and Rosedale Roads, Albany, Auckland 1310, New Zealand (a division of Pearson New Zealand Ltd)
Penguin Books (South Africa) (Pty) Ltd, 24 Sturdee Avenue, Rosebank, Johannesburg 2196, South Africa

Penguin Books Ltd, Registered Offices: 80 Strand, London WC2R 0RL, England

www.penguin.com

First published in New Zealand by Mallinson Rendel Publishers Limited 1989
First published in Great Britain in Puffin Books 1991
Reissued in 2005
40

Made and printed in Italy by Printer Trento Srl

British Library Cataloguing in Publication Data
A CIP catalogue record for this book is available from the British Library

ISBN-13: 978-0-14054-240-0